9/33

A+
books

DINOSAUR FACT DIG

IGUANODON
AND OTHER BIRD-FOOTED DINOSAURS
THE NEED-TO-KNOW FACTS

BY
JANET RIEHECKY

Consultant: Mathew J. Wedel, PhD
Associate Professor
Western University of Health Services

CAPSTONE PRESS
a capstone imprint

A+ Books are published by Capstone Press,
1710 Roe Crest Drive, North Mankato, Minnesota 56003
www.mycapstone.com

Library of Congress Cataloging-in-Publication Data
Names: Riehecky, Janet, 1953- author.
Title: Iguanodon and other bird-footed dinosaurs : the need-to-know facts /
by Janet Riehecky.
Description: North Mankato, Minnesota : Capstone Press, [2017] | Series: A+
books. Dinosaur fact dig | Audience: Ages 6-8. | Audience: K to grade 3. | Includes
bibliographical references and index.
Identifiers: LCCN 2015048107| ISBN 9781515726968 (library binding) | ISBN
9781515727002 (pbk.) | ISBN 9781515727040 (ebook (pdf))
Subjects: LCSH: Iguanodon–Juvenile literature. | Dinosaurs–Juvenile literature.
Classification: LCC QE862.O65 R53 2017 | DDC 567.914–dc23
LC record available at http://lccn.loc.gov/2015048107

EDITORIAL CREDITS:

Michelle Hasselius, editor; Kazuko Collins, designer; Wanda Winch, media researcher;
Gene Bentdahl, production specialist

IMAGE CREDITS: All images by Jon Hughes except: MapArt (maps), Shutterstock: Elena
Elisseeva, green gingko leaf, Jiang Hongyan, yellow gingko leaf, Taigi, paper background

Printed in China.
022016   007586

**NOTE TO PARENTS, TEACHERS,
AND LIBRARIANS:**

This Dinosaur Fact Dig book uses
full-color images and a nonfiction
format to introduce the concept of
bird-footed dinosaurs. *Iguanodon and
Other Bird-Footed Dinosaurs* is designed
to be read aloud to a pre-reader or to
be read independently by an early reader.
Images help listeners and early readers
understand the text and concepts discussed.
The book encourages further learning by
including the following sections: Table of
Contents, Glossary, Critical Thinking Using
the Common Core, Read More, Internet
Sites, and Index. Early readers may need
assistance using these features.

TABLE OF CONTENTS

Iguanodon and other bird-footed dinosaurs were herbivores that used their hard beaks and teeth to eat plants. Dinosaurs in this group could walk on two legs. But they could also drop down on all four legs to eat low-growing plants.

Bird-footed dinosaurs did not have long claws or armor to protect them. Instead many dinosaurs in this group ran away from predators. These dinosaurs also lived in herds. Predators were less likely to attack a large group of dinosaurs. Read on to learn more about Iguanodon and other bird-footed dinosaurs.

ABRICTOSAURUS

PRONOUNCED: ab-RICK-tuh-SAWR-us

NAME MEANING: wide-awake lizard

TIME PERIOD LIVED: Early Jurassic Period

LENGTH: 4 feet (1.2 meters)

WEIGHT: 90 to 100 pounds
(41 to 45 kilograms)

TYPE OF EATER: herbivore

PHYSICAL FEATURES: long tail;
large hands; sharp, pointed beak

ABRICTOSAURUS was one of
the first dinosaurs found that had
different kinds of teeth in its mouth.

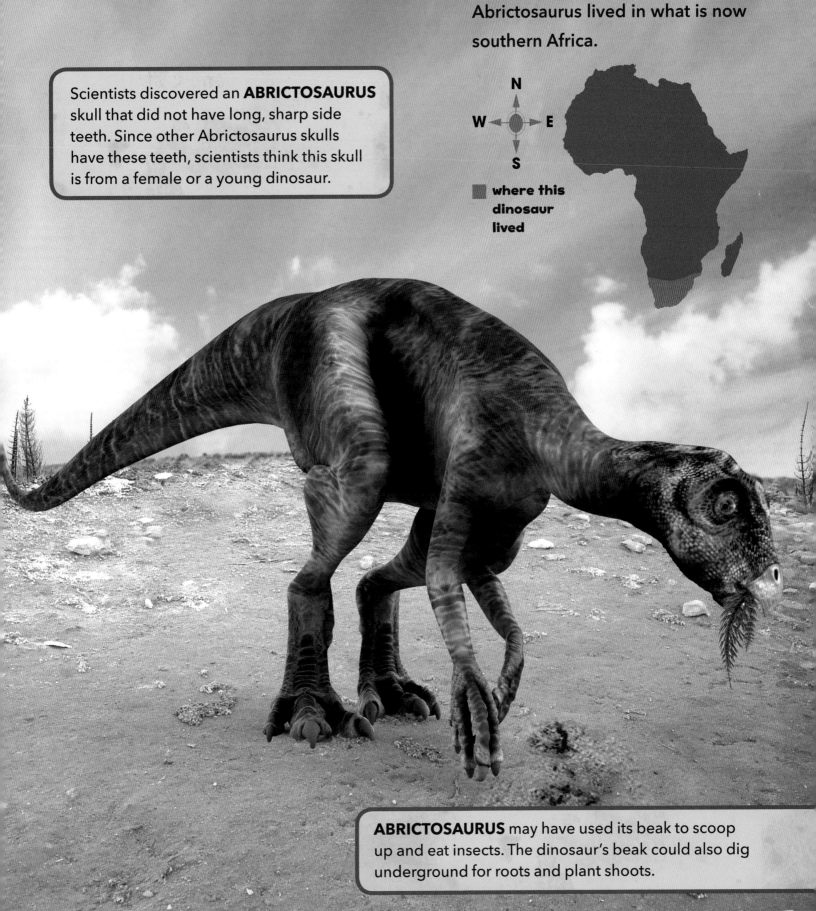

Scientists discovered an **ABRICTOSAURUS** skull that did not have long, sharp side teeth. Since other Abrictosaurus skulls have these teeth, scientists think this skull is from a female or a young dinosaur.

Abrictosaurus lived in what is now southern Africa.

N
W E
S

■ where this dinosaur lived

ABRICTOSAURUS may have used its beak to scoop up and eat insects. The dinosaur's beak could also dig underground for roots and plant shoots.

GASPARINISAURA

PRONOUNCED: GAS-pih-RIN-eh-SAWR-uh

NAME MEANING: Gasparini's lizard; named after paleontologist Zulma Brandoni de Gasparini

TIME PERIOD LIVED: Late Cretaceous Period

LENGTH: 2.1 feet (0.6 m)

WEIGHT: 5 pounds (2.3 kg)

TYPE OF EATER: herbivore

PHYSICAL FEATURES: long, thick tail; long feet; short head

GASPARINISAURA swallowed rocks to help it digest plants. The rocks helped break down the plants into tiny pieces.

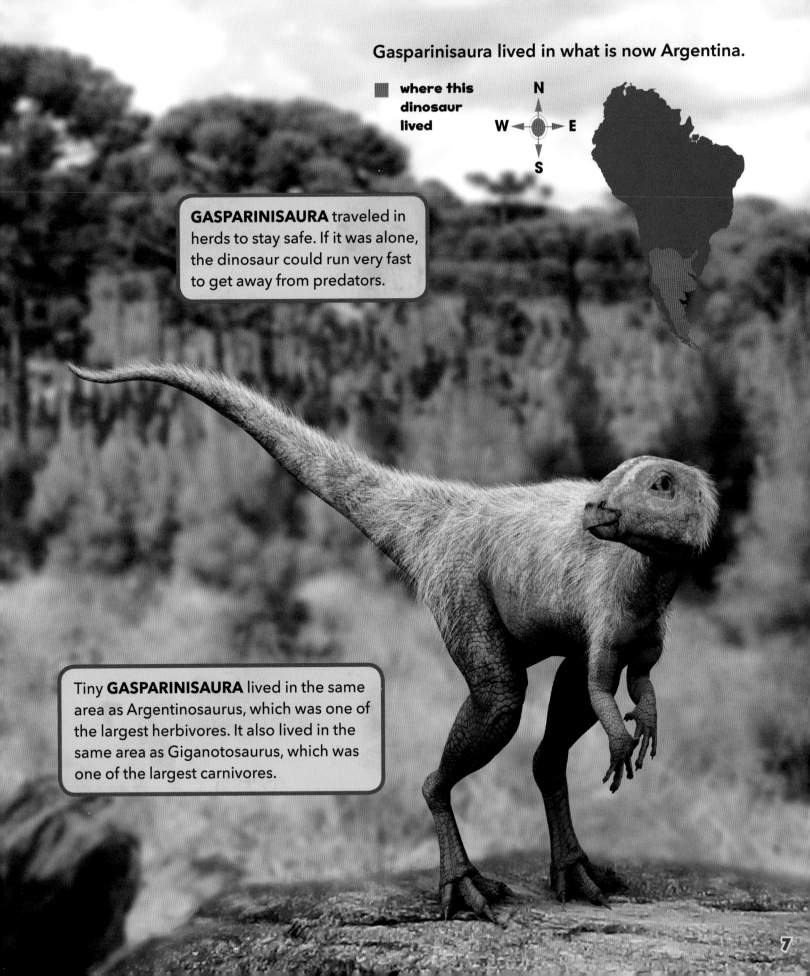

Gasparinisaura lived in what is now Argentina.

■ where this dinosaur lived

N
W ← → E
S

GASPARINISAURA traveled in herds to stay safe. If it was alone, the dinosaur could run very fast to get away from predators.

Tiny **GASPARINISAURA** lived in the same area as Argentinosaurus, which was one of the largest herbivores. It also lived in the same area as Giganotosaurus, which was one of the largest carnivores.

HEXINLUSAURUS

PRONOUNCED: HEX-in-luh-SAWR-us

NAME MEANING: named after Professor He Xin-Lu from the Chengdu University of Technology in China

TIME PERIOD LIVED: Middle Jurassic Period

LENGTH: 6 feet (1.8 m)

WEIGHT: 20 to 50 pounds (9 to 23 kg)

TYPE OF EATER: herbivore

PHYSICAL FEATURES: thick tail; long legs; short arms

Hexinlusaurus lived in an area with shallow lakes in what is now central China.

N
W E
S

□ **where this dinosaur lived**

Scientists had a hard time deciding what kind of dinosaur **HEXINLUSAURUS** was. They thought its fossils could be from Yangdusaurus, Agilisaurus, and Proyandusaurus.

HEXINLUSAURUS' fossils are at the Zigong Dinosaur Museum in Dashanpu, China.

Scientists have only found HEXINLUSAURUS' skull and a few bones so far.

9

HYPSILOPHODON

PRONOUNCED: HIP-sih-LOF-uh-don

NAME MEANING: high-ridged tooth

TIME PERIOD LIVED: Early Cretaceous Period

LENGTH: 5.9 feet (1.8 m)

WEIGHT: 20 to 50 pounds (9 to 23 kg)

TYPE OF EATER: herbivore

PHYSICAL FEATURES: five fingers on each hand; large eyes; wide, leaf-shaped teeth

Scientists have found **HYPSILOPHODON** nests with carefully arranged eggs. This might mean the dinosaur took care of its young.

At first scientists thought **HYPSILOPHODON** lived in trees. Now scientists know it lived on land.

Hypsilophodon lived near rivers, lakes, and swamps in what is now western Europe and Alberta, Canada.

N
W E
S

where this dinosaur lived

When **HYPSILOPHODON** closed its mouth, its top teeth slid over the outside of its bottom teeth like scissors. Every time the dinosaur opened or closed its mouth, it sharpened its teeth.

IGUANODON

PRONOUNCED: ih-GWAN-o-dahn

NAME MEANING: iguana tooth

TIME PERIOD LIVED: Early Cretaceous Period

LENGTH: 30 feet (9 m)

WEIGHT: 3.5 tons (3.2 metric tons)

TYPE OF EATER: herbivore

PHYSICAL FEATURES: stiff tail used for balance; sharp spikes for thumbs; leaf-shaped teeth

At first scientists thought **IGUANODON** had a spike on its nose. Now scientists know it had spikes instead of thumbs. The dinosaur could use its thumb spikes to stab at food or to protect itself.

Close relatives of **IGUANODON** have
been found in North America, Africa,
Asia, and Australia.

IGUANODON was the second
dinosaur to be named.

IGUANODON had teeth on the sides of its mouth. The dinosaur could use these teeth to chew up plants.

IGUANODON became extinct about 125 million years ago.

IGUANODON could walk on two or four legs, similar to a kangaroo today.

IGUANODON was discovered in 1822. The dinosaur's giant teeth were stuck in the rocks near Sussex, England.

Iguanodon lived in woodlands in what is now Europe.

N
W E
S

where this dinosaur lived

LEAELLYNASAURA

PRONOUNCED: lee-EL-in-a-SAWR-ah

NAME MEANING: Leaellyn's lizard; named after the daughter of paleontologists Patricia Vickers-Rich and Thomas Rich

TIME PERIOD LIVED: Early Cretaceous Period

LENGTH: 3 feet (0.9 m)

WEIGHT: 5 to 20 pounds (2 to 9 kg)

TYPE OF EATER: herbivore

PHYSICAL FEATURES: very long tail; bone that stuck out above eyes; huge eyes

LEAELLYNASAURA lived in a place that got very cold during the winter. The sun did not come up for three months. Some scientists think this means the dinosaur was warm-blooded.

LEAELLYNASAURA had huge eyes. Some scientists think the dinosaur could see in the dark.

Leaellynasaura lived in forests in what is now southern Australia.

N
W E
S

where this dinosaur lived

LEAELLYNASAURA had better eyesight than any other dinosaur in this group.

MUTTABURRASAURUS

PRONOUNCED: MUT-uh-BUR-uh-SAWR-us

NAME MEANING: named after the town of Muttaburra in Australia, where fossils were found

TIME PERIOD LIVED: Early Cretaceous Period

LENGTH: 29.5 feet (9 m)

WEIGHT: 1 to 4 tons (0.9 to 3.6 metric tons)

TYPE OF EATER: herbivore

PHYSICAL FEATURES: long tail; powerful jaw; sharp teeth; long, rounded nose

MUTTABURRASAURUS had a large, hollow space inside its nose. Some scientists think the space helped the dinosaur smell. Others think the dinosaur used it to make loud sounds.

Scientists made casts of **MUTTABURRASAURUS'** bones and put them together. It was the first Australian dinosaur to be put on display.

Muttaburrasaurus lived in conifer forests in what is now Australia.

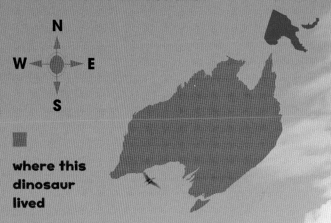

where this dinosaur lived

Humans and most animals lose one tooth at a time. **MUTTABURRASAURUS** lost a whole row of teeth. A new row of teeth was waiting underneath to replace it.

ORYCTODROMEUS

PRONOUNCED: or-ICK-to-DROH-me-us

NAME MEANING: digging runner

TIME PERIOD LIVED: middle Cretaceous Period

LENGTH: 7 feet (2 m)

WEIGHT: 50 to 100 pounds (23 to 45 kg)

TYPE OF EATER: herbivore

PHYSICAL FEATURES: tail that bent easily; strong legs; powerful shoulder muscles; broad, horned beak

ORYCTODROMEUS took care of its young until they were fully grown.

Oryctodromeus lived in dry woodlands in what is now Montana.

N
W   E
S

■ where this dinosaur lived

ORYCTODROMEUS dug underground burrows to lay its eggs. The eggs would be safe from dangerous weather and predators that couldn't fit inside.

Scientists found small side tunnels connected to **ORYCTODROMEUS'** underground burrows. This shows insects or other small creatures shared the dinosaur's burrows.

OURANOSAURUS

PRONOUNCED: oo-RAN-uh-SAWR-us

NAME MEANING: brave lizard

TIME PERIOD LIVED: Early Cretaceous Period

LENGTH: 19.7 feet (6 m)

WEIGHT: 1 to 4 tons (0.9 to 3.6 metric tons)

TYPE OF EATER: herbivore

PHYSICAL FEATURES: strong legs; narrow sail on its back; small, rounded horns; long beak

OURANOSAURUS may have been hunted by the giant crocodile Sarchsuchus. Sarchsuchus was almost 40 feet (12 m) long. Scientists nicknamed it "SuperCroc."

Ouranosaurus lived in the forests and swamps of what is now Niger, Africa.

N
W E
S

☐ where this dinosaur lived

OURANOSAURUS had thumb spikes, similar to Iguanodon.

OURANOSAURUS' sail was held up by long, wide spines. Some of the spines were almost 2 feet (0.6 m) long.

THESCELOSAURUS

PRONOUNCED: THES-ki-lo-SAWR-us

NAME MEANING: marvelous lizard

TIME PERIOD LIVED: Late Cretaceous Period

LENGTH: 13 feet (4 m)

WEIGHT: 500 to 600 pounds (227 to 272 kg)

TYPE OF EATER: herbivore

PHYSICAL FEATURES: long, powerful legs; wide back; short arms; small head

THESCELOSAURUS was one of the last dinosaurs to become extinct.

Thescelosaurus lived in what is now the northwestern United States. It also lived in southwestern Canada.

N
W ✦ E
S

where this
dinosaur
lived

THESCELOSAURUS weighed about as much as a pony today.

A **THESCELOSAURUS** skeleton was found in 1993. At first scientists thought they had found the dinosaur's fossilized heart in its chest. Later scientists discovered it was just a strange-shaped rock.

XIAOSAURUS

PRONOUNCED: ZEE-ah-oh-SAWR-us

NAME MEANING: dawn lizard

TIME PERIOD LIVED: Middle Jurassic Period

LENGTH: 3 feet (0.9 m)

WEIGHT: 5 to 20 pounds (2 to 9 kg)

TYPE OF EATER: herbivore

PHYSICAL FEATURES: thin body; short arms; small claws; small head

Construction workers building a parking lot uncovered thousands of dinosaur bones in 1979. **XIAOSAURUS** was found in the same place four years later.

Xiaosaurus lived in what is now central China.

N
W E
S

where this dinosaur lived

Besides **XIAOSAURUS'** fossils, giant long-necked dinosaurs and big carnivores have been found in Dashanpu, China.

The names **XIAOSAURUS** and Eosaurus both mean "dawn lizard." Eosaurus was a reptile that lived in the sea but is now extinct.

ZEPHYROSAURUS

PRONOUNCED: ZEF-i-ruh-SAWR-us

NAME MEANING: west wind lizard; Zephyros is the god of the west wind in Greek mythology

TIME PERIOD LIVED: Early Cretaceous Period

LENGTH: 6 feet (1.8 m)

WEIGHT: 20 to 50 pounds (9 to 23 kg)

TYPE OF EATER: herbivore

PHYSICAL FEATURES: long tail; short arms; small head; beak

ZEPHYROSAURUS lived during the same time period as Deinonychus, a fierce raptor.

Many dinosaurs could only move their jaws up and down to chew. **ZEPHYROSAURUS** could move its jaw up and down and side to side.

Zephyrosaurus lived near the rivers and swamps of what is now western North America.

N
W E
S

where this dinosaur lived

ZEPHYROSAURUS may have made footprints discovered in Maryland and Virginia.

GLOSSARY

BEAK (BEEK)—the hard part of a bird's mouth; some dinosaurs had beaks

BURROW (BUHR-oh)—a tunnel or hole in the ground made or used by an animal

CARNIVORE (KAR-nuh-vor)—an animal that eats only meat

CONIFER (KON-uh-fur)—a tree with cones and narrow leaves called needles

CRETACEOUS PERIOD (krah-TAY-shus PIHR-ee-uhd)—the third period of the Mesozoic Era; the Cretaceous Period was from 145 to 65 million years ago

EXTINCT (ik-STINGKT)—no longer living; an extinct animal is one that has died out, with no more of its kind

FOSSIL (FOSS-uhl)—the remains of an animal or plant from millions of years ago that have turned to rock

HERBIVORE (HUR-buh-vor)—an animal that eats only plants

HERD (HURD)—a large group of animals that lives or travels together

HOLLOW (HOL-oh)—empty on the inside

JURASSIC PERIOD (ju-RASS-ik PIHR-ee-uhd)—the second period of the Mesozoic Era; the Jurassic Period was from 200 to 145 million years ago

PALEONTOLOGIST (pale-ee-uhn-TOL-uh-jist)—a scientist who studies fossils

PREDATOR (PRED-uh-tur)—an animal that hunts other animals for food

PRONOUNCE (proh-NOUNSS)—to say a word in a certain way

RELATIVE (REL-uh-tive)—a member of a family

SPIKE (SPIKE)—a sharp, pointy object

SPINE (SPINE)—the backbone of an animal

WARM-BLOODED (WARM BLUHD-id)—animals that have a body temperature that remains the same, no matter their surroundings; birds and mammals are warm-blooded

CRITICAL THINKING USING THE COMMON CORE

1. Name two dinosaurs that lived in the same area as Gasparinisaura. (Key Ideas and Details)

2. Scientists believe Leaellynasaura could have been warm-blooded. What does "warm-blooded" mean? (Craft and Structure)

3. What was unusual about the place where Xiaosaurus' bones were discovered? (Key Ideas and Details)

READ MORE

Hughes, Catherine D. *First Big Book of Dinosaurs.* National Geographic Little Kids. Washington, D.C.: National Geographic, 2011.

Lee, Sally. *Iguanodon.* Little Paleontologist. North Mankato, Minn.: Capstone Press, 2015.

Raatma, Lucia. *Iguanodon.* Dinosaurs. Ann Arbor, Mich.: Cherry Lake Pub., 2013.

INTERNET SITES

FactHound offers a safe, fun way to find Internet sites related to this book. All of the sites on FactHound have been researched by our staff.

Here's all you do:

Visit *www.facthound.com*

Type in this code: 9781515726968

Super-cool stuff!

Check out projects, games and lots more at **www.capstonekids.com**

INDEX